For my mother, Johanna Oelschläger Carle

PUFFIN BOOKS

Published by the Penguin Group
Penguin Books Ltd, 80 Strand, London WC2R 0RL, England
Penguin Group (USA) Inc., 375 Hudson Street, New York, New York 10014, USA
Penguin Group (Canada), 90 Eglinton Avenue East, Suite 700, Toronto, Ontario, Canada M4P 2Y3
Penguin Ireland, 25 St Stephen's Green, Dublin 2, Ireland
Penguin Books Australia Ltd, 707 Collins Street, Melbourne, Victoria 3008, Australia
Penguin Books India Pvt Ltd, 11 Community Centre, Panchsheel Park, New Delhi – 110 017, India
Penguin Group (NZ), cnr Airborne and Rosedale Roads, Albany, Auckland 1310, New Zealand
Penguin Books (South Africa) (Pty) Ltd, Block D, Rosebank Office Park, 181 Jan Smuts Avenue,
Parktown North, Gauteng 2193, South Africa
Penguin Books Ltd, Registered Offices: 80 Strand, London WC2R 0RL, England

puffinbooks.com

First published by Philomel Books, a division of Penguin Group (USA), Inc., 2004
Published in Great Britain in Puffin Books 2004
Published in this edition 2006
012

Copyright © Eric Carle, 2004
Eric Carle's name and his signature logo type are trademarks of Eric Carle
All rights reserved

The moral right of the author/illustrator has been asserted

Set in GillSans. The artwork was done in painted tissue-paper collage

Manufactured in China

British Library Cataloguing in Publication Data
A CIP catalogue record for this book is available from the British Library

ISBN 978-0-14056-989-6

To find out more about Eric Carle, visit his web site at www.eric-carle.com

ERIC CARLE
MISTER SEAHORSE

PUFFIN

Mr and Mrs Seahorse drifted gently through the sea.
Mrs Seahorse began to wiggle and twist, this way and that.

"It's time for me to lay my eggs," she said.
"Can I help?" asked Mr Seahorse.
"Oh, yes. Thank you!" said Mrs Seahorse
and she laid her eggs into a pouch on Mr Seahorse's belly.
"I'll take good care of our eggs," said Mr Seahorse,
"I promise."

As Mr Seahorse drifted gently through the sea,
he passed right by . . .

As Mr Seahorse drifted gently through the sea,
he passed right by . . .

a lionfish hidden behind a coral reef.

But before long, Mr Seahorse met another fish.
"How are you, Mr Tilapia?" asked Mr Seahorse.
Mr Tilapia couldn't answer. His mouth was full of eggs.
"I know, I know," said Mr Seahorse. "Mrs Tilapia has laid her eggs.
Now you are taking good care of them until they hatch."
Mr Tilapia nodded his head.
"You must be very happy," said Mr Seahorse
and swam on his way.

As Mr Seahorse drifted gently through the sea,
he passed right by . . .

a pair of leaf fish hidden among the seaweed.

But before long, Mr Seahorse met another fish.
"How are you, Mr Kurtus?" asked Mr Seahorse.
"Perfectly fine," replied Mr Kurtus.
"Mrs Kurtus has laid her eggs and I have stuck them on my head.
Now I am taking good care of them until they hatch."
"You are doing a good job," said Mr Seahorse
and swam on his way.

As Mr Seahorse drifted gently through the sea,
he passed right by . . .

a stonefish hidden behind a rock.

But before long, Mr Seahorse met another fish.
"How are you, Mr Pipe?" asked Mr Seahorse.
"Couldn't be better," replied Mr Pipe.
"Mrs Pipe has laid her eggs along my belly.
Now I am taking good care of them until they hatch."
"You should feel proud of yourself," said Mr Seahorse
and swam on his way.

But before long, Mr Seahorse met another fish.
"How are you, Mr Bullhead?" asked Mr Seahorse.
"Tip-top," replied Mr Bullhead.
"Mrs Bullhead laid her eggs, the eggs hatched.
Now I'm babysitting."
"You are doing a great job," said Mr Seahorse
and swam on his way.

The time had come for the seahorse babies to be born.
Mr Seahorse wiggled and twisted, this way and that.
At last, the babies tumbled out of Mr Seahorse's pouch
and swam away.

One baby turned around and tried to get back into the pouch.
"Oh, no!" said Mr Seahorse. "I *do* love you,
but now you are ready to be on your own."